Smithsonian Prehistoric Zone

Spinosaurus

by Gerry Bailey
Illustrated by Chris Scalf with Gabe McIntosh

Crabtree Publishing Company

www.crabtreebooks.com

Crabtree Publishing Company

www.crabtreebooks.com

Author
Gerry Bailey

Illustrators
Chris Scalf
Gabe McIntosh

Editorial coordinator
Kathy Middleton

Editor
Lynn Peppas

Proofreaders
Reagan Miller
Kathy Middleton

Prepress technician
Samara Parent

Print and production coordinator
Katherine Berti

Copyright © 2010 Palm Publishing LLC and the Smithsonian Institution, Washington DC, 20560 USA
All rights reserved.

Spinosaurus, originally published as *Spinosaurus in the Storm* by Ben Nussbaum, Illustrated by Chris Scalf with Gabe McIntosh
Book copyright © 2005 Trudy Corporation and the Smithsonian Institution, Washington DC 20560.

Library of Congress Cataloging-in-Publication Data

Bailey, Gerry.
 Spinosaurus / by Gerry Bailey ; illustrated by Chris Scalf and Gabe McIntosh.
     p. cm. -- (Smithsonian prehistoric zone)
 Includes index.
 ISBN 978-0-7787-1815-4 (pbk. : alk. paper) -- ISBN 978-0-7787-1802-4 (reinforced library binding : alk. paper) -- ISBN 978-1-4271-9706-1 (electronic (pdf)
 1. Spinosaurus--Juvenile literature. I. Scalf, Chris. II. McIntosh, Gabe. III. Title. IV. Series.

 QE862.S3B358 2011
 567.912--dc22

                         2010044031

Library and Archives Canada Cataloguing in Publication

Bailey, Gerry
   Spinosaurus / by Gerry Bailey ; illustrated by
Chris Scalf and Gabe McIntosh.

(Smithsonian prehistoric zone)
Includes index.
At head of title: Smithsonian Institution.
Issued also in electronic format.
ISBN 978-0-7787-1802-4 (bound).-- ISBN 978-0-7787-1815-4 (pbk.)

        1. Spinosaurus--Juvenile literature. I. Scalf, Chris
II. McIntosh, Gabe III. Smithsonian Institution
IV. Title. V. Series: Bailey, Gerry. Smithsonian prehistoric zone.

QE862.S3B338 2011   j567.912   C2010-906886-6

Crabtree Publishing Company

www.crabtreebooks.com   1-800-387-7650
Copyright © **2011 CRABTREE PUBLISHING COMPANY**.

Published in the United States
Crabtree Publishing
PMB 59051
350 Fifth Avenue, 59th Floor
New York, New York 10118

Published in Canada
Crabtree Publishing
616 Welland Ave.
St. Catharines, Ontario
L2M 5V6

Printed in China/012011/GW20101014

Dinosaurs

Living things had been around for billions of years before dinosaurs **evolved**. Animal life on Earth started with single-cell **organisms** that lived in the seas. About 380 million years ago, some animals came out of the sea and onto land. These were the ancestors that would become the mighty dinosaurs.

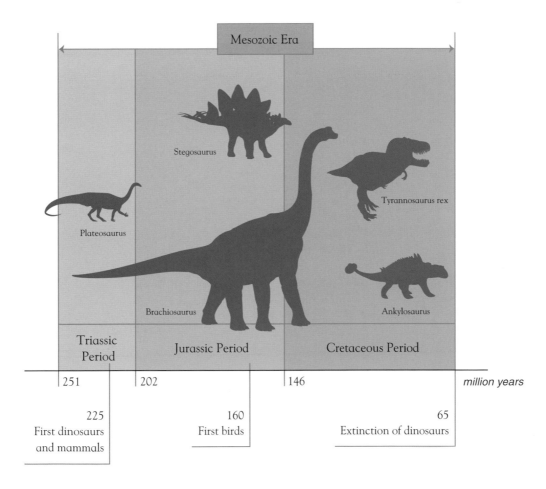

The dinosaur era is called the Mesozoic era. It is divided into three parts called the Triassic, Jurassic, and Cretaceous periods. During the Cretaceous period flowering plants grew for the first time. Plant-eating dinosaurs, such as *Paralititan*, roamed the land. Meat-eaters, such as *Spinosaurus* and *Velociraptor*, fed on the plant-eaters and other dinosaurs. By the end of the Cretaceous period, dinosaurs (except birds) had been wiped out. No one is exactly sure why.

The huge Spinosaurus had not slept well.
It had rained heavily all night. The sound
of crashing waves and the cries of the
leather-winged pterosaurs gliding above
the **mangrove** forest had woken him.
The air felt cool and humid even though
it was early morning. He opened his jaws
and yawned to show his sharp teeth.
He was a dangerous **predator**.

Spinosaurus got to his feet and looked around.
Water lay everywhere. It was 95 million years
ago in what is now North Africa. It was the place
where a mighty river gushed into the ocean.

The river had now flooded its banks and the
tides were higher than ever. He would have
to find drier ground and wait until the floods
went down. If he did not, he might drown.

Spinosaurus made huge footprints in the mud as he slowly walked inland. The rain was coming down harder now, but he could not speed up. He was a cold-blooded animal and he needed sunshine to warm his blood.

Without this warmth reaching the wide sail
shape on his back, he did not have his usual
energy. He plodded on because he had to
get out of the flooded **bog**.

Other animals scurried by as he made his way inland.
They were looking for drier ground too. Small dinosaurs
such as these usually were a tasty meal for Spinosaurus,
as well as the odd fish he could catch by the shore.

But he was not interested in eating
right now. He would worry about
that later when he felt safe from
the flooding.

At last Spinosaurus felt firm ground under his feet. The rain stopped and he felt the sun on his back. It warmed him and dried his skin.

The clouds had disappeared for now. This would
be a good place to wait until the floods had gone
down. Then he would go back to the seashore.

But today, Spinosaurus was in for a surprise.
He suddenly heard the loud sound of footsteps
crashing through the forest. It was another
Spinosaurus like himself but larger.

It had reached the firm ground
ahead of him. It was not interested in
sharing. It **loomed** over Spinosaurus,
huge and angry.

The giant dinosaur reared up angrily
and roared. It glared at Spinosaurus.
Its yellow eyes flashed with rage. The
smaller Spinosaurus stood his ground.

The two creatures snarled at
each other, showing rows of
long, sharp teeth. Neither one
was going to back down.

Spinosaurus knew he had a chance if he could scare away the larger dinosaur. He did not want to fight. He raised himself as high as he could, but he was a young dinosaur and not as tall as the other one. Suddenly the larger dinosaur lunged.

It caught Spinosaurus's sail in its mouth, which sent a flash of pain along his back. At the same time the bigger dinosaur raked a claw across his body and opened a small wound.

Spinosaurus had to act quickly. He knew
he could not win a fight. This dinosaur
was just too big. He would have to back
down. Quickly he turned and ran.

He would continue his journey inland and find a place that was not taken by someone bigger and stronger than he was. The rain still held off and the sun shone brightly through the misty forest air.

21

At last Spinosaurus came to a stream. He was not alone. There was a giant plant-eater called Paralititan. It lived in the mangrove forest and was eating there. He could also see the tracks of a large meat-eater called Bahariasaurus. He would have to watch out for that creature. But the tracks were old. The vegetation he moved through was rich, and there were signs of life everywhere. He would not starve here.

Spinosaurus was starting to feel tired now. He needed to take a break so he lay down. He made sure his sail was sideways to the sun. Luckily, the other Spinosaurus had not done a lot of damage. He would heal quickly.

He was in a safe place now, and he would settle and rest here. Only after he felt stronger would he return to his home near the shore.

All about Spinosaurus

(SPINE-oh-SORE-us)

Spinosaurus lived during the Cretaceous period about 95 million years ago. It lived near tropical swamps across what is now North Africa. Scientists do not know a great deal about the world in which *Spinosaurus* lived. Only a few dinosaurs that lived alongside *Spinosaurus* have been found.

Some scientists think that *Spinosaurus* was a fish-eater, and used its long jaws to snatch fish out of the water. It may also have used its strong arms and long claws to catch and hold onto fish and other **prey** animals. It would have walked upright on its hind legs.

It had long jaws for eating meat or fish. Its teeth were straight, not curved like most **carnivores** of its type.

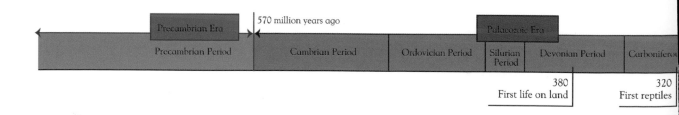

Precambrian Era		570 million years ago			Palaeozoic Era		
Precambrian Period		Cambrian Period	Ordovician Period	Silurian Period	Devonian Period		Carboniferou

380
First life on land

320
First reptiles

Spinosaurus was up to 39 feet (12 meters) long which made it one of the largest carnivores. Its most **distinctive** feature was a huge sail on its back. The sail was made up of long spines that rose almost seven feet (2 meters) from its back. The sail may have been covered in a layer of skin or muscle.

No one knows exactly what this sail was used for. Some scientists believe it was used to help control the *Spinosaurus*'s body temperature. The sail had a lot of **blood vessels** inside it. When the *Spinosaurus* turned its sail sideways to the sun, the surface of it would heat up quickly. The warmed-up blood would be pumped around its body. The animal would angle its sail away from the sun to cool down. Other scientists believe the sail was used for **display** or to threaten other *Spinosaurus*. It is possible it was used for both these purposes.

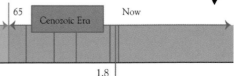

Period	Permian Period	Triassic Period	Jurassic Period	Cretaceous Period		Cenozoic Era	Now

248

Mesozoic Era

65

1.8
First humans

Footprints

Spinosaurus created huge footprints as he made his way inland. He had already left a trail of these by the shore. What he did not know was that these footprints would be **preserved** as **fossils**. They were discovered millions of years later.

Scientists who study dinosaurs are called paleontologists. They use these fossils to figure out a dinosaur's **structure**, how it walked, and how fast it traveled. They can also tell whether a dinosaur hunted alone or in packs. Large meat-eaters, for example, usually traveled alone.

Scientists know that some dinosaurs walked on their toes and held their legs directly under their body by studying their tracks.

Some dinosaurs walked on four legs and were called quadrupeds. Others walked on two legs and were called bipeds. Dinosaur tracks also show that these animals did not drag their tails on the ground but held them up for balance.

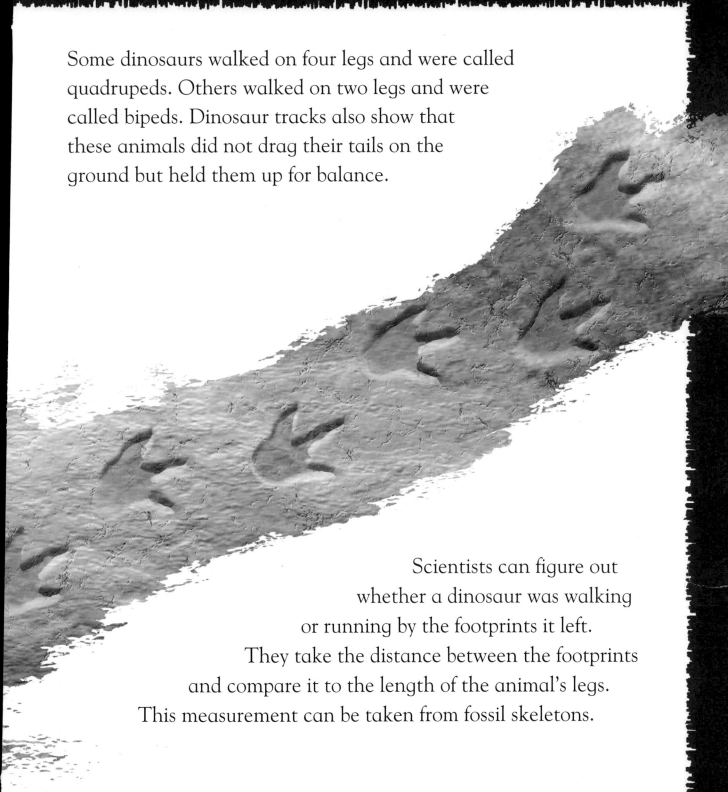

Scientists can figure out whether a dinosaur was walking or running by the footprints it left. They take the distance between the footprints and compare it to the length of the animal's legs. This measurement can be taken from fossil skeletons.

Warm blood or cold blood?

When dinosaur remains were first discovered, scientists believed they were cold-blooded animals, as present-day lizards and snakes are. A cold-blooded animal controls its body heat by using its **environment**. For example, it can warm or cool its blood by moving in and out of the sun during the day.

A warm-blooded animal, such as a human or other mammal, depends mostly on food energy to make body heat. To lose heat, a warm-blooded animal sweats or pants. Some, such as elephants, flap their ears to cool the blood flowing through them.

Animals can become too cool or too hot to **function**. It is important that they have a way of controlling their temperature.

Cold-blooded?

Were the dinosaurs cold-blooded? You can save a lot of energy by simply using the sun to warm up your body instead of having to go and hunt for food. So some scientists believe dinosaurs used this method. Dinosaurs also lived in a hotter world than we do, which may have helped them stay warm.

If *Spinosaurus* was cold-blooded, it might have used the huge sail on its back to heat up its blood by turning it toward the sun. If it wanted to cool down, it would turn its sail away from the sun and into shadow.

Warm-blooded?

Others argue that dinosaurs were warm-blooded, that creatures such as the huge *Apatosaurus* could not warm up in the sun because it would take too long to warm up such a large body. And the small, **sickle**-clawed *Velociraptor* could not have maintained such an active life unless it was warm-blooded.

If *Spinosaurus* was warm-blooded, it would not have needed the sun for warmth at all. Maybe its sail was actually used to show colors to a mate or to make it look more threatening.

Glossary

blood vessel A channel or canal that carries blood throughout a living body

bog Wet, swampy area of ground

carnivore A meat-eater, or animal that feeds on another animal's flesh

display To show so that others see

distinctive Having a different or special characteristic that others do not have

environment The natural conditions in which an organism lives

evolve To grow and change through time

fossil The hardened remains of an organism that lived thousands of years ago

function To perform a normal activity

loom To rise above as a large, threatening shape

mangrove A tropical forest that grows along tidal shores

organisms Any living plant or animal

predator An animal that hunts other animals for food

preserve To protect or remain without change

prey An animal that is hunted by another animal for food

sickle A sharp, knife-like object with an outwardly rounded blade

structure The parts of something that altogether form the whole thing

tide The changing levels of the oceans caused by the gravitational pull of the moon and sun

Index

Apatosaurus 31
Bahariasaurus 22
body temperature 27, 28
biped 29
claws 19, 26
cold-blooded 8, 30, 31
Cretaceous Period 3, 26
fish 10, 26
flood 7, 9, 11, 13

footprints 8, 28, 29
fossil 28, 29
jaws 4, 26
Jurassic period 3
meat-eater 3, 22, 28
Mesozoic era 3
North Africa 6, 26
paleontologist 28
Paralititan 22
plant-eater 3, 22

predator 4
pterosaur 4
quadruped 29
sail 9, 19, 24, 26, 27, 31
spine 26
teeth 4, 17, 26
tracks 22, 28, 29
Triassic period 3
Velociraptor 3, 31
warm-blooded 30, 31

Further Reading and Websites

Spinosaurus by Susan Heinrichs Gray. Child's World (2004)

Spinosaurus by Daniel Cohen. Capstone Press (2000)

Websites:

www.smithsonianeducation.org